Lost and Alone, I Need a Home!

To Jenny

Graci Hartman

Graci Hartman

Palmetto Publishing Group
Charleston, SC

First Edition

Printed in the United States.

ISBN-13: 978-1-64111-251-2
ISBN-10: 1-64111-251-4

Lost and Alone

I Need A Home

story by
Graci Hartman

I'm fuzzy on the details.

This is all I know:

I was lost and very scared,

With no place to go.

Cars were all around me;
There were buildings, big and tall,
With many doors and windows,
And I was oh-so-small!

Then I heard a soft voice,

So gentle, warm, and kind.

"Over here!"

she called to me.

What a surprise, I did find!

Water and some tasty food,
Much to my delight.
I was very hungry
And gobbled up every bite!

Nestled in the carrier,

Riding in the car,

"We have to see the vet," she said.

"It isn't very far."

He checked me over, up and down.

"It's a boy you have," said the vet.

I was happy to hear him say,

"He's healthy.

What a wonderful pet!"

She took me back to her small house.

I was warm, safe, and dry.

I heard her say, "He needs a home.

All we can do is try!"

She also said, "I'd like to keep him,

But that would never do,

Because I'm allergic to cats...

"AH-CHOO!"

People came, both day and night.

They didn't visit long,

Until the daughter with her Mom,

Who wanted to take me home.

"He needs a name," the mother said.

"He's as cute as it gets!

How about Tom, or Fred, or Bob—

I know, let's call him

Fritz!"

Fritz, it is! I like that name!

It suits me very well.

A name . . . a home . . . people all my own.

I will like this, I can tell!

So . . .

In the carrier and to the car,

To my home, where I will stay.

I was lost, but now I'm found;

All I can say is,

"YAY!"